DRAFTS

RADHIKA JOSHI SHAH

ISBN 979-888503998-7

Contents

Preface v

1. Teenage Girl & Mother 1
2. Unborn Child & Mom To Be 3
3. Wife & Husband 5
4. Grandma & Grand Child 8
5. To Best Friend 10
6. Go Ahead ! 12
7. Life's Teaching 14
8. Darkness 15
9. Madness In Friendship 16
10. Mistreat 17
11. Love 18
12. Friendship 19
13. Mumbai Life 20
14. I Miss You 21
15. Words Are Powerful 22
16. Even If 23
17. Smile 24
18. Need & Care 25
19. Bike Rider Quotes 26

Preface

This book is collection of unsent letters, short tales and quotes dedicated to bike riders. We can not express our feelings everytime even if we actually want to convey to the person. Some feelings forever stay in our heart and never come out. This book let's you introduce such untold feelings in the form of letters that may relate to your side of story or it may give you insight to feel your loved one's feelings for you. Here, I have written some short tales too. Honestly, it is not just a piece of words, it is the phase of life that taught some unforgettable lesson and turned you a person you're today. I don't believe in drafts. You must heart out your feelings. You never know how much a heart can hold. Unsaid feelings hurt the most. Don't regret by keeping the drafts. Just send it ! Write it ! and be free of the burden you hold from long time. Breath freely !

CHAPTER ONE

Teenage Girl & Mother

Letter to a teenage girl from mother to make her understand the world with the eyes of experienced mother. Just a try to introduce her daughter a harsh reality of people and how to deal with it.

Dear Sakshi ,

It has been long time we have not get time to talk. Do you remember when we last interacted?

So I thought about to try this traditional way to reach out to you. You are grown up now and you know what is right and wrong. But as a mother, I could not stop myself to care for you. In this world of showing up, people are hiding the ugly truth behind the fake social media presence. They show up how they have better lifestyle than you. And you may get attracted towards such a people and believing false information. There are times you feel less privileged in terms of Independence, money or luxuries. You may fall for wrong person. You may get hurt badly from your beloved ones, betrayed by

best friends, cheated by someone. It happened!

Always remember that " Your last mistake is your best teacher." Never loose your principles

to answer the fools. Be careful about your ethics. Do not loose your confidence when others try to see exactly broken you ! Be good to everyone but never accept anyone to hurt your feelings.

Your self respect is your biggest asset. You do not have to compromise it again and again. The person who broke your heart is the one who does not deserve you. Forgive people often but do not forget the lesson you learned from it. If you feel uncomfortable by any means, you must trust your parents and open up about your situation. Whenever you feel depressed, you must know your mother-father is always there for you. You know dear, I can be your trusted secret keeper.

I know you are such a strong girl but if anytime you feel that you are getting weak at the moment and can't survive the situation, I am just call away my girl ! I see you as my junior version and want it to see you always rocking my darling !

Lots of love to you !

From,

Your Mummy.

CHAPTER TWO

Unborn Child & Mom to be

Heart touching letter of pregnant woman to her unborn child. She described her situation, her mood swings and tell her baby to do not get affected by it

To My Baby,

Baccha your mumma loves you so much. Ummm sometimes your mumma is getting hyper, sad & crying
but you must know your mumma is so strong . Yes there comes a time in life when me too get upset with people, can't handle the bad vibes, feeling uneasy...

And waiting for your arrival, please do not get affected by unpleasant vibes. Mumma is trying hard to keep you safe from all bad vibes, thinking and surrounding so sometimes mumma get stressed...

But you know na your mumma is smile smile, Happy and deal with everything strongly. You have to learn to deal with the situation and do not loose your charm. Do not let world to change your smile. Just ignore the people who disturb your peace of mind and drain your energy.

Be with people who really cares for you. The people who make u smile and do not let your precious tears to fall down. Make few friends but for lifetime - The real gems.

Do not bother about others who remembers you when they are in need and disappears once their intention is fulfilled.

I want you to prepare from now when you are in tummy because this world is game, and we never know when it makes us winner or looser. It is ok to loose but it is not ok to give up my child! You have to be prepare for all the time. Do not show your weakness to world, I am always here to
convert your weaknesses into strength. Your smile, Your character, Your eyes, Your achievements makes you the person you always wanted to be ! This world does not care about how far you came and from where? It only understands who is on the top ? Be a bigger person but
do not forget the roots. Stay grounded, humble and powerful.
Waiting to Welcome You !

From,
Yours Mumma

CHAPTER THREE

Wife & Husband

Newly married couple : A wife writes a letter to her husband to express her feelings and want him to know her as a person

Dear Aaditya,

I know, I took a lot of time to reply your letter. It has been 5 months and today I decided to
write you. I am not so introvert person. Mostly I choose not to show my feelings because I have
experienced the immense pain when someone play with your feelings. So better to take time to show
your true feelings and that I did.

On the day we met , I learned that we both are having very different personalities. Our choices may be
same but our thought process is very different from each other. I am free spirited, imperfect and
charming. I like to be around the people who are having easy going attitude towards life. I can't live in
stressful situations created by the people who wantsto keep us in their control. Basically I want to live my
life with my own interests. I do not consider myself as a perfect human being. So please accept me whenever I will make some

silly mistakes.

I must say you are mature, sensible person whereas I am childish and emotional person. I think this will balance us to be a best couple.

See we get married in arranged marriage so please give me sometime. Falling in love is happened itself. I can't do it purposely. I will take some time to understand each other bit more. First I want to be your best friend and then after our mutual understanding, love, care , relationship will grow. And you know what " Relationships are made strong with time not forcefully ". And I am sure our bond will be the strongest one.

When we started dating each other as fiance, it was just a memorable time . That time gave us cheerful memories. Spending some time together before marriage is only ensure us about how much we can share and enjoy together. But when we committed for lifetime includes other people in our life too. We have to adjust others. Sometimes it is possible and sometimes I can't. Respect is give and take aspect of life. Right?
You are too good I know. You give respect to everyone even if you can't get the same. You do sacrifice your happiness for the sake of others.

We are not same ! I am not that good as I can't respect those who insult others. I do not make any sacrifices for the people who do not value you or me. I am very straightforward by my words and my thoughts, principles.

I am not saying to change you but I expect to understand my way of thinking also.

Everyone is not just like you ! We met different people in the journey of life . Everyone is special in
their own way. We just need to accept it or let go. It does not mean we should permit others to hurt our
feelings. If you feel happy to serve people who do not deserve actually, you continue but please do not
make me a part of it.

As a wife, my responsibility is to keep your head high and do not let anyone to misuse you

or take advantage of your goodness. I just expect little support from your end to.

When son take a stand for his mother, he is a good boy !

When son take a stand for his wife, he is bad boy !

This is theparameters set by this system which is very wrong ! Please speak up when you feel something wrong is done with me. Otherwise I have to take stand for myself and you know I could do it.

I wish we try to know eachother much more and be the ideal husband wife . You are

obedient son and I respect it always! Let's be a best couple too !

Yours,
Mitali.

CHAPTER FOUR

Grandma & Grand Child

A girl write a letter for her Grandma. Her Grandma is passed away and she is missing her a lot. She do not know how to express her feelings so she write it out in the remembrance of her Grandma

Dear Grandma,

I miss you so much. Why you left me so soon ? You were my best friend. I am feeling too
lonely without you. I was so lucky that I had you as my Grandma. You supported me, loved me and
cared for me a lot. When mom went out for office, whole day you had taken care of me, played with me, fed me. I am missing our mischief, our laughter, our ice cream party. Why you left so soon...

Now I am a big girl and this is your dream to see me successful one. Today I have everything , I achieved a lot in life by your grace and blessings but you are not with me. This hurts me a lot. People say every wound is curable with time but I can't forget the pain of loosing you suddenly. I made many friends. I met many people. But the attachment we share is unique. Actually I never feel to make best friends when you are in my life. Because I know I can share anything and everythingwith my Grandma. And the worst day of my life came, when I got the message to come home fast. Itis urgent. When I came.... I saw the crowd at the gate and then you are still body on the bed. It was just unbelievable that how can you left me like this?

Those days were so painful. Slowly slowly I get back to life but Grandma, I am still in pain.

I know you are watching me from the heaven. You keep your eyes on me. I am sure you must be happy watching me growing, achieving and working hard. I miss you at every stage of my life .

When I defeated, I want you to encourage me.
When I achieved, I want to see your smiling face.
When I sad , I want your warmth to make me comfortable.

I just wish to have you as my Grandma in every life. I never want to stay away from you. Love y0u and
miss you a lot.

Yours,
Gudiya

CHAPTER FIVE

To Best Friend

Breaking up in Friendship is very painful. It changes us as a person. This draft is for long lost friend who is no more in contact but not forgotten

Dear BFF,

Yes Bff Best friend forever ! Even after your betrayal I never given this tag to anyone in my life.
You can say I am not interested to make anyone this much important. I hope you are happy in your life
right now. I do not know anything about you from past 6 years. Yeah when you left me in pieces, I ran
behind you, chased you and beg to you for our friendship but at that time your ego, your anger is on
the top. You hurted me a lot dear ! I was so stupid and childish when I used to run behind you and did many things that are against my beliefs. Your continuous ignorance, insulting me and your rough treatment made me a most robust person. Do you remember I have done little things to make you happy, just to see you smiling. You know I can do anything for your happiness. I was so much involved in friendship that I forgot my worth.

I loved you so much but today I hate you a lot because you made me a person exactly opposite to original me ! It is so bad to hurt someone at the extent that they have to leave their true nature. I have affected a lot by the way you behaved on my mistakes. I came to you just to ask forgiveness. I ran behind you a lot. I begged a lot. Why can't you forgive me? You treated me like craps. And you know my words could be bitter but I never behaved the bad like you. I am also human being. I have feelings too. One day I lost the patience and we lost respect for each other. From that day we never cross the paths. You know what, if I can ask for punishment for you, I will say " You will never get a friend like me" . Yes dear because you never imagine how much I adore you and how badly you changed my love into the negativity. I am writing this today because I want to make myself free from this negative emotion. I just do not want any feeling associated with you. I just want to let you go and be at distant. When I remembered those time, I found myself full of love and charm. However, you have changed me in wrong ways. It's ok ! Now, I do not want to take that load of bad emotions and grief. I want to free myself. You can't control my ability to love. You have already damage the part of me but now it's enough ! Just break the cord and leave. I wish you can live your life the way you want. This is the last time I called you Bff. Henceforth we are just a stranger that never going to meet !

Final Goodbye !

Yours,
Nothing.

CHAPTER SIX

Go Ahead !

Life is one way road, you can look back and
smile/cry but you can't go back, you can't change it !
We may find our clear vision bit late than others but
it's ok !

We realised now we should do that little early.

We should take some decisions earlier in life.

We have wasted some years, we did some mistakes !

Take it as lesson !

Take it as experience !

Don't feel guilty for anything, just keep in mind tonever repeat the same pattern !

Forgive yourself & go ahead !

Don't let any Kash....to ruin your present !

What is gone is gone !

What you have now is everything you can do with !

Yeah just grab this moment !

Take chances !

Make choices that you always want to choose but
you scared to talk about your passion because of
Log kya kahenge... !

Once u start to walk on ur path u will reach eventually to destination after passing all the
troubles, cross all the stones, let it bleed ur feet but
you must keep walking !

We choose profession to earn money that's prior !
Very few can prioritise between money & passion !
Earn money but keep your passion alive !
Do what keep you satisfied, happy, fullfilled while earning!
Work is worship ! Make your talent to be used !
Your talent beats your degree when your dream something different, something unique, when you don't want only money but you want name & fame too !
Trust your instincts ! ♥
Take risks !
It's never too late to work on our passion !
Face challenges ! Be creative ! Think out of box !
Learn from it ! Dream big & make it true !
Start is always from tiny step !
Trust yourself !
Trust on God that he is watching your efforts !
Important is just Start it !
Be the best version of yourself !

CHAPTER SEVEN

Life's Teaching

Life teaches us in every step..
The moment when you start trusting someone
blindly....
That person breaks you..!
When you expect your silence to be
understood.. ..
people take your words wrong..!
Gestures are not important even
though shown heartily....
but fake words are appreciated..!
So, do not make anyone your life....
Do not be affected by anyone's absence or
presence....
Because when you face darkness it's you
all alone who faces it..!

Trust yourself
Value yourself
Love yourself....

CHAPTER EIGHT

Darkness

Darkness is not about scare us always.
Sometimes it becomes your secret keeper !
It allows you to shade tears which you don't
want to show to the world !
It accepts you at your lonely hours and
strengthens you to face the light after big loss !
Darkness has its own version that protects you
from the outside fears.

CHAPTER NINE

Madness in Friendship

कही मैं देर से पोहंचु तो याद आता है,
कभी मैं वक्त से पेहले भी जाया करता था !

That time...that feelings...when you never want to be late , even if you are not well, there is heavy rain outside, or any other reason that will suggest you to not to go...
And still you desperately find your way just to be there without being late...just because you don't want to miss that meet, that moments, that

craziness, that comfort zone, never want to loose in any condition... that madness !

As time passes people changed, our feelings may not change but our words, our action turned to be completely opposite !
We never feel to cross the road with them again... because we did lot before and we didn't want to suffer again...!

Still we suffer by memories we had with them !
After all

"SUFFERING IS PERSONAL, LET OURSELVES TO SUFFER !"

CHAPTER TEN

Mistreat

When people mistreat you, you must not ignore it....

When someone cross your patience limit,
Answer them back !

First, they Dislike you..
Then, they Hate you...
And
Finally, they wish to never see your face again !

Here you Win !
When they didn't spare any way to go out of their life, make them to go out of yours !
Don't let anyone harm your self respect !

CHAPTER ELEVEN

Love

Love is not about physical intimacy, it's all about Emotional Intimacy...

Love is when you can't see each other but still can feel each other
You can feel pain in that smile, can hear silence without words...

Love is when you make feel comfortable to someone just being there...
Love is when you don't give advices, only your presence is enough...
Love is when just one stare make heartbeat faster...

Love is so deep...so pure...

CHAPTER TWELVE

Friendship

Friendship has lots of power
It makes you to do things that you could not imagine you can do !
It keeps your confidence high !
It never lets you feel failed or useless, it can see beyond imperfections !
It makes you smile at your hardest !
It wipes your tears at your weakest !
It has been and will be with you at all your even and odds !
It gives you strength to go ahead when you can't even put your feet step to out of door !
It makes you smile , laugh and feel complete when you are not even bother about what's next !
Very Few ! The gems I got are irreplaceable ever !

CHAPTER THIRTEEN

Mumbai Life

Year in Mumbai, changes the whole attitude towards life !
From "Easy" travel to "Fast & Furious"
From "Sharp 9 AM" to "Sharp 8:44" every minutes count...
From "Easy bus travel" to "Challenging train travel"
From "Attachments" to "Professional"

Yes people always running to make dreams true.. Enthusiasm...

Forget the concept of "Log kya kahege?" Everyone has their own goals, reason of living, own dreams, own struggles.

Learned a lot about how to be strong and dedicated towards your goal in any condition never fall emotionally.

Be stable. Be strong.

CHAPTER FOURTEEN

I Miss You

I miss you....
When I trapped between the people who don't allow me to take my decision!
You always give me freedom to what I wanted to do.
I miss you....
When I want to share the deepest secrets !
You never have judged me for my falling
I miss you....
When I just have to cover face by fake smile !
You were the one who could read my crying heart
I miss you....
When I just want to take break and no one could understand my discomfort
You were there to let me wander in my own world
I wish we would meet life after life...
And this time for not being apart...

CHAPTER FIFTEEN

Words are Powerful

Words are so powerful, it can heal you or hurt you. As time passes we learned to control our words even if we want it to say it loudly and in as ugly as we felt because of that particular person or situation. We learned to stay away such toxicity of people which decreases our goodness, love we carry in our heart, kindness, peace of mind.

Don't let others to harm your purity, your affection, your ability to see positives in every worse situation ! Keep distance from their existence directly or indirectly in your lives !

They are narcissistic ! That they often confused between what they want or don't want !
They keep grudges !
They don't know the idea of love so they transform our love to their type of negative energy and trying to drain us !

Beware of such narcissistic people which is more dangerous to your emotional health !
Hope they will find the right direction and get a life that they don't have time to look into the other's life !

CHAPTER SIXTEEN

Even If

Even if it is unsaid, truth always wins.

Even if you are not allowed to talk, your gratitude towards them is unchanged.

Even if you skip arguments because of respect, you are at your best.

Even if they talk strict to you, you know they have that right on you.

Sometimes they are unaware of all the facts and they only believe on one side of story,

So sometimes when you are not allowed to talk is actually their acceptance of your side also but they can't choose one of the side.

It actually feels like a win win situation, when you chooseto loose your argument, keep your values, request tolisten politely and get no permission to stand for your side of story, still you have same calm feeling for them because you respect the person more than anything.

CHAPTER SEVENTEEN

Smile

Your past has gone.
Your future is yet to come.
Whatever you have is present. So cheer up.
Whatever happened, is happened.
Whatever is going to happen, will happen.
Stop thinking too much.
Stop cursing your life.
You are doing good.
You deserved to be loved.
Enjoy the present moment. Cheer up. Dance. Sing. Have fun
Love life. Live life.

CHAPTER EIGHTEEN

Need & Care

Express yourself to someone who cares for you,
Not to someone who needs you....
Because "*CARE*" is a Personal Commitment
"*NEED*" is a Personal Requirement.

CHAPTER NINETEEN

Bike Rider Quotes

These quotes are dedicated to passionate bike riders who love to ride bikes in inferior situation and face challanges to reach at the destination. Writer tried to sum of the story of bike rider in two liners.

Bike Riding is a Passion

Friendship is all about you & me !
You never left me on the difficult paths where I needed you the most.

Never mess with me
I am Rider with Style, Smile and Attitude !

Sometimes looking back and smile towards past
is good.
Afterall it makes you the person you are today !

My heart is beating for you !
Yes, you are my forever love ♥

Don't allow anyone to let your flame down !
You are the rider with fire !

Very peaceful :
Such a dark evening with my bike !

Don't walk away !
Instead take a ride and forget the world for a while

Loving yourself is the nicest !
Standing alone is the strongest !
Riding with confidence is the bravest !

Loving yourself is the nicest !
Standing alone is the strongest !
Riding with confidence is the bravest !

Explore the places !
Get lost & get find !
Feel the thrills !

Before my destiny changes my destination,
I reach there !

Bro ! Come on !
Together we could be the best at facing challenges

Way to infinite journey by leaving the world behind !

At the times
When I want to be far from crowd !
My bike is the best companion to spend time with !

Life is short !
Dont waste it spending at one place
Go out ! Explore ! Enjoy !

Don’t try to catch me !
I am addicted to wandering

Printed by Libri Plureos GmbH in Hamburg,
Germany